Two by Duras

Two by Duras

Marguerite Duras

Translated by
Alberto Manguel

Coach House Press
Toronto

L'Homme atlantique was originally published in
1982 by Les Éditions de Minuit
La Pute de la côte normande was originally published in
1986 by Les Éditions de Minuit
Copyright © 1982, 1986 by Les Éditions de Minuit
Interview copyright © 1993 by Ana María Moix
Translation copyright © 1993 by Alberto Manguel

This book was published with the assistance
of the Department of Communications,
the Ontario Arts Council and
the Ontario Publishing Centre.

Canadian Cataloguing in Publication Data
Duras, Marguerite
     Two
ISBN 0-88910-441-7
I. Title.
PQ2607.U845T96 1993   843'.914   C93-093449-0

Contents

The Slut of the Normandy Coast

...Luc Bondy had asked me to direct *La Maladie de la mort* (*The Malady of Death*) at the Schaubühne in Berlin. I had accepted, but I had told him that first I'd have to adapt it for the stage, that I'd have to make a selection of the text, that it could be read but not acted. I made the adaptation. In it, the protagonists were silent, and the actors were the ones who told their story, what they had said, what had happened to them.

All the scenes, all ten or twelve of them, were finished. They were to be read, as well as the text of the dialogue between the main characters. The woman had not been called upon in this adaptation, she had been set aside. It was about the man, not the woman. Two days after having sent this stage adaptation of *La Maladie de la mort* to Berlin, I phoned to ask them to send it back because I no longer wanted to do it. I told Yann. I often tell him what I'm doing. As soon as I had been dispossessed of the manuscript, I realized I had made a mistake. I had done exactly what I had tried to avoid. I had gone back to *La Maladie de la mort,* to its very principle of a text for three voices, to its stilted and unitary form. I had been emptied out, I had become the opposite of a writer. I was the plaything of a formal fate from which I was trying unsuccessfully to escape. I spoke of this to Yann. He didn't believe me. He had often seen me stalled in my projects, come to a halt, then begin again. Three times I started on the Berlin adaptation, the third time with a typist and a schedule. That time I dictated what I imagined to be the perfect version, but in fact it was the worst of all, pompous and artificial. Three times I tried. I

would begin with *La Maladie de la mort*
and I would come back to it. While I
was working I had no idea where I was
going. I'd find myself back there, each
time back to the same place in the
book, huddled against it, dazed. I could
no longer trust myself, I was lost. To
make matters worse, it was always at
the stage of typing out the final draft
that I would become aware of the
results. Whatever I did, it seemed that I
had always to resort to a false solution:
the stage. Once again I spoke to Yann. I
told him it was over. I was fed up with
wasting time, I was giving up the idea
of adapting the text. I said that I

discovered, once again, that *La Maladie de la mort* was such an evidently ambiguous text that one had to use other methods to subdue it, and there was nothing I could do about it. This is still all I know about the difficulties I had with that text.

And then there was that Quilleboeuf episode, to which I paid no attention at the time. Shortly afterwards, I began a book that was to be called *L'Homme menti* (*The Perjured Man*), but was also abandoned. And then, one day, the weather was warm, in the evening, at night. It was midsummer, in June. I began writing about the summer, about the hot evenings. I didn't know exactly why, but I carried on.

It is the summer of 1986. I'm writing the story. Throughout the summer, every day, sometimes in the evening, sometimes at night. It is then that Yann enters a period of crying out loud, of shouting. He types out the book, two hours a day. In the book, I'm eighteen, I'm in love with a man who loathes my desire, my body. Yann types as I dictate. While he types, he doesn't shout. That happens afterwards.

He shouts at me, he becomes a man demanding something, who doesn't know what that something is. So he shouts, to say that he doesn't know what he wants. And he also shouts to find out, so that, from the current of words, the knowledge of what he wants might appear on its own. He can't separate the detail of what he wants this summer from the whole of what he has always wanted. I hardly ever see him, this man, Yann. He's hardly ever there, in our apartment by the sea. He goes for walks. During the day he covers different distances, each several times. He goes from hill to hill. He visits the large hotels, he seeks out beautiful men. He meets several handsome bartenders. Also on the golf courses he seeks them out. He sits in the lobby of the Hôtel du Golf and waits there, watching. That evening he says, 'I had a nice quiet time at the Hôtel du Golf, I felt very relaxed.' Sometimes he falls asleep in the Hôtel du Golf lounge chairs, but, as he's well-dressed, very elegant, Yann, all in white, they let him sleep. He carries with him all the time a huge old blue bag, made out of cloth, which I made in case he needed it for his shopping. He keeps his money there. At night, he goes to the Melody. In the afternoons he also goes, sometimes, to the Normandy. In Trouville, he goes to the Bellevue. When he comes back, he screams, he shouts at me, and I carry on writing. Even if I say, 'Hello', 'How are you?', 'Have you had dinner?', 'Are you tired?', he shouts.

Every night, for a month, he wants the car to drive to Caen and see some friends. I refuse to give him the car because I'm afraid. So he takes taxis, he becomes the driver's chum, his best client. When he shouts, I continue to write. At first, it was difficult. I thought it was unfair, his shouting at me. That it wasn't right. And when I wrote and saw him coming and knew that he was going to shout, I could no longer write, or rather the writing stopped everywhere. There was nothing left to write, and I would write sentences, words, scribbles, to make believe that I didn't hear the shouting. I spent weeks with a jumble of different writings. Today I believe that those that seemed to me then the most incoherent were, in fact, the most decisive in the book to come. But of this I knew nothing. I wouldn't tell him that I couldn't write because of his shouting, and because of what I thought was his unfairness towards me. Soon, even when he wasn't there, I was incapable of writing. I waited for his shouts, his screams, but I continued to fill the page with sentences that were alien to the book that was there, in the process of being made, in a field foreign to it, in fiction.

At last a sense of order was established, one for which I was not responsible, I who worked the writing onto the page, but for which Yann was responsible, he alone, and without putting pen to paper, without having to do anything about it, without any other intention than that of slaughtering, down to its very roots, anything that might be seen as an encouragement to live on. Of himself and of his anger he knew as little as an animal does, that is to say, nothing, not even that he shouted. That is how, a month before the date agreed upon for the delivery of the manuscript, I began the definitive book, that is to say, I began to find that man, Yann, not where he really was, but by seeking him in things that were alien to both him and the book—for instance, in the landscapes of the Seine estuary. Very much there. And in himself as well, in his smile, Yann's smile, in his walk, his hands, Yann's hands.

I separated him completely from his words, as if he had caught them unwittingly, and they had made him ill. And that was how I found out that he was

right. That he was right to want something with such intensity, whatever it
might be. However terrible it might be.
Sometimes I would imagine that the
time had come, that I was going to die.
Four years ago I underwent a treatment
that left me weak; since then I tend to
believe that death is there, within reach
of my life. He wanted everything at
once, he wanted to destroy the book
and he feared for the book's survival.
For weeks he had typed two hours a
day for me. Drafts, different stages of
the book. He knew that the book was
already in existence. He would say,
'What the fuck are you doing writing

all the time all day long? You've been abandoned by everyone. You're crazy, you're the slut of the Normandy coast, a fool, you're embarrassing.' After that, sometimes we'd laugh. He was afraid I'd die before the book was completed, maybe, or rather, that I'd throw the book away, once again.

I no longer thought about Quilleboeuf, but I still felt the need to go there. I would go there with friends, but I didn't know why that alien place meant so much to me; I thought it was because of the large river that ran past the square where a café stood. I thought that it was because of the sky of Siam, here yellow with petrol fumes, while Siam itself was dead.

Sometimes he would return at five in the morning, happy. I began not to ask him any more questions, not to speak to him, to say good morning just for the pleasure of doing so. Then he became louder, he became terrible, and at times I was afraid, and believed that he was more and more in the right, but I could no longer stop the book, any more than he could stop the violence. I'm not certain against what Yann was shouting. I think it was against the book itself, real or imagined, beyond all definition, pretext, excuse, etc. It was simply that: making a book. It went beyond what was reasonable in its reasons, and what was unreasonable in those same reasons. It was like a goal: kill it. I knew that. I knew more and more things about Yann. In the end, it was like a race. Run faster than him in order to finish the book, so that he would not stop it completely. I lived with this throughout the summer. I also must have expected it. I would complain to people, but not about the essentials, not about what I am writing now. Because I thought that they would not be able to understand. Because there had been nothing in my entire life as illicit as our story, Yann's and mine. It was a story that meant nothing outside our space, the space where we stood.

It's impossible to speak of how Yann spent his time, his summer—it's impossible. He had become unreadable, unpredictable. One could say that he had become fathomless. He went in all directions, to all those hotels, to search beyond the beautiful men, the bartenders, the husky bartenders of foreign lands, of Argentina or Cuba. He spun in all directions. Yann. All directions met in him at the end of the day, at night. They met in the mad hope that a scandal might occur, an absolutely commonplace scandal centred around my own life. In the end, it began to be readable. We had reached a place where life was not totally absent. Sometimes we received signals from it. It, life, strolled along the seaside. Sometimes it crossed through town, in the cars of the Morality Squad. There were also tides, and then Quilleboeuf, of which one became aware, in the distance, as ever-present as Yann.

When I wrote *La Maladie de la mort*, I did not know how to write about Yann. That I know. Here, the reader will say, 'What's got into her? Nothing happened, since nothing takes place.'

When in fact what took place is what happened. And, when nothing else takes place, then the story is truly beyond the reach of both the writer and the reader.

The Atlantic Man

You will not look straight at the camera. Except when you are told to do so.

    You will forget.
    You will forget.

    You will forget that this is you.
    I believe it can be done.
    You will also forget the camera. But
above all, you will forget that this is
you. You.

Yes, I believe it can be done. For instance, from other points of view, the point of view of death among others, your death, lost somewhere in the midst of a nameless and pervasive death.

You will look at what you see. But you will look at it absolutely. You will try to look at it until your sight fails, until it makes itself blind, and even through this blindness you must try again to look. Until the end.

You ask me: look at what?
I say, well, I say 'the sea,' yes, this

word facing you, these walls facing the
sea, these successive disappearances, this
dog, this coast, this bird beneath the
Atlantic wind.

Listen. I also believe that if you were
not to look at that which appears before
you, it would become apparent on the
screen. And the screen would go blank.

What you would see there——the sea,
the window-panes, the wall, the sea
beyond the window-panes, the windows in the walls——all things are things
that you have never seen before, never
looked at before.

You will think that this, which is about to take place, is not a rehearsal, that this is a first night, just as your life itself is a first night as every second unfolds. That among the millions of men hurling themselves to their death throughout the ages, you are the only one to stand for himself, in my presence, at this very moment of the film that is being made.

You will think that it is I who have chosen you. I. You. You who are at every moment all of you, beside me, and this is true whatever you do, however far or near you might be from my hopes.

You will think about your own self, but in the same way as you think about this wall, this sea that has not yet taken place, that wind and that gull separated for the very first time, that lost dog.

You will think the miracle is not in the apparent similarity between each of the particles that make up those millions of men in their continuous hurling, but in the irreductible difference that separates them from each other, that separates men from dogs, dogs from film, sand from the sea, God from the dog or from that tenacious gull struggling against the wind, from the liquid crystal of your eyes, from the sharp crystal of the sands, from the unbreathable foul air in the hall of that hotel after the dazzling light of the beach, from each word, from each sentence, from each line in each book, from each day and each century and each eternity past or future, and from you and from me.

During your stay you must believe in your inalienable majesty.

You will proceed. You will walk as you do when you are alone and when you believe someone is watching you, I or God, or that dog along the sea, or that tragic gull braving the wind, so alone in the presence of the Atlantic element.

I wanted to say: film believes it can preserve what you are doing at this moment. But you, from where you are, wherever it may be, whether you have gone away still bonded to the sand, or the wind, or the sea, or the wall, or the bird, or the dog, you will realize that film cannot do that.

Go on to something else. Give up.
Proceed.

You will see, everything will come
from your walking along the sea,
beyond the pillars in the hall, from the
movements of your body that you had,
until now, thought natural.

You will turn right and walk along
the window-panes and the sea, the sea
behind the window-panes, the windows
in the walls, the gull, and the wind, and
the dog.

You have done it.

You are on the edge of the sea, you are on the edge of those things trapped among themselves by your eyes.

Now the sea is to your left. You can hear its murmur mingled with the wind.
In huge strides it advances towards you, towards the dunes on the coast.

You and the sea, you are but one for me, one single object, the object of my role in this adventure. I too look at it. You must look at it as I do, as I look at it, with all my power, from where you are.

You have left the camera's field of view.

You are absent.

With your leaving, your absence has taken over, it has been photographed just as your presence was photographed a little while ago.

Your life has distanced itself.

Only your absence remains now, bodyless, without any possibility of reaching it, of falling prey to desire.

You are precisely nowhere.
You are no longer the chosen one.

Nothing remains of you except this floating absence, ambulatory, that fills the screen, that peoples by itself, why not? a prairie in the Far West, or this abandoned hotel, or these sands.

Nothing happens except this absence drowned in regret and which, at this point, leaves nothing to weep for.
Don't let yourself be overcome by these tears, by this sadness.

No.

Continue to forget, to ignore the future of all this, and also your own future.

Last night, after your final departure, I went into the room on the ground floor, the room that opens onto the park, there where I always go during the tragic month of June, the month that leads into winter.

I had swept the house, I had cleaned

everything as thoroughly as if preparing for my funeral. Everything had been cleared of life, exempted, emptied of traces, and then I said to myself: I'll start to write, in order to cure myself of the lie of this love affair that is ending. I washed my things, only a few things, and everything was clean, my body, my hair, my clothes, and also their enclosure: these rooms, this house, this park.

And then I started to write.

When everything was ready for my death, I began to write about what you've never understood, knowing that you would never understand. That's how it happens. I always address myself to your lack of understanding. Without that, you see, it wouldn't be worthwhile.

But suddenly I cared little for that impossibility of yours, I would leave it in your hands, I'd have no part of it, I'd give it back to you, my wish being that you take it with you, that you make it part of your dreams, part of the decomposing dream you were told was happiness—I mean the decay of the mutual happiness of lovers.

And the day returned as usual, in tears, and ready for the performance.

And once again, the performance took place.

And instead of dying, I went out onto the terrace in the park and without emotion I called out loud the date of that day, Monday June fifteenth, 1981, that day you left in the dreadful heat, forever, and I believed, this time yes, that it was forever.

I think I didn't suffer from your leaving. Everything was as usual, the trees, the roses, the turning shadow of the house on the terrace, the time and date, and yet you, you, you were absent.

I didn't think that you had to come back. Around the park, the doves on the rooftops called out to their mates to join them. And then it was seven in the evening.

I told myself that I would have loved you. I thought that by then all that was left to me of you was nothing more than a hesitant memory, but no, I was wrong. My eyes remembered those beaches, a place to kiss and a place to lie on the warm sand, and that look of yours so focused on death.

That was when I said to myself, why

not? Why not make a film? From now on writing would be too difficult. Why not a film?

And then the sun rose. A bird crossed the terrace along the wall of the house. Thinking the house empty, it flew so close that it grazed one of the roses, one of the roses I call 'of Versailles.' The movement was violent, the only movement in that park under the even light in the sky. I heard the bird's brushing of the rose in its velvet flight. And I looked at the rose. The rose stirred as if imbued with life, and then little by little, became again an ordinary rose.

You have remained in the state of having left. And I have made a film out of your absence.

You will pass once again in front of the camera. This time you will look at it.

Look at the camera.

The camera will now capture your reappearance in the mirror parallel to that in which it sees itself.

Don't move. Wait. Don't be surprised. I'll tell you this: you will reappear in the image. No, I didn't warn you. Yes, it will happen again.

Now you already have, behind you, a past, a plan.
Now you already have grown old.

Now you already are in danger. Now your greatest danger is resembling yourself, resembling the man in that first shot taken an hour ago.

Forget more.
Forget even more.

You will look at all the people in the audience, one by one, each one in particular.

Remember this, very clearly: the movie-theatre is in itself, like yourself, the entire world, you are the entire world, you, you alone. Never forget that.

Don't be afraid.

No one, no other person in the world can do what you will now do: pass by this place a second time today, under my orders alone, before God.

Don't try to understand that photo-graphic phenomenon, life.

This time, you will die as you look on.

You will look at the camera as you looked at the sea, as you looked at the sea and the window-panes and the dog and the tragic bird in the wind and the still sands braving the waves.

At the end of the journey, the cam-era will have decided what you will have looked at. Look. The camera won't lie. But look at it as if it were an object of choice determined by yourself, something for which you have always waited, as if you had decided to face it at last, to engage with it in a struggle of life and death.

Act as if you had just now understood, as you held it in your eyes, that it was this, the camera, that at first had wanted to kill you.

Look around you. As far as the eye can see you will recognize these barren stretches of sand, these valleys held together by wars and by happiness, these valleys of film, they look at one another, face one another.

Turn away.
Walk on.
Forget.
Walk away from that detail, the cinema.

The film will remain like this. Finished. You are at once hidden and present. Present only through the film, beyond this film, hidden from yourself, from all knowledge anyone could have of you.

While I no longer love you I no longer love anything, nothing, except you, still.

Tonight it's raining. It's raining around the house and on the sea. The film will remain like this, as it is. I have no more images for it. I no longer know where we are, at what end of what love, at what beginning of what other love, in what story we have lost ourselves. It is only for this film that I know. For the film alone I know, I know, I know that no image, no single image more, could make it last any longer.

Light hasn't broken all day long and there isn't the slightest breeze in the treetops of the forests, or in the fields, the valleys. No one knows if it's still summer or the end of summer, or some other deceitful, undecided season, ugly, nameless.

I no longer love you like I did on the first day. I no longer love you.

Nevertheless, those expanses around your eyes remain, always there, and the life that stirs you in your sleep.
There also remains that exaltation that comes over me from not knowing what to do with all this, with the knowledge I have of your eyes, of the immensities your eyes explore, to the

point of not knowing what to write, what to say, what to show of their pristine insignificance. Of those things I only know this: that I have nothing to do now except suffer that exaltation about someone who once was here, someone who was not aware of being alive and whom I knew was alive,

of someone who didn't know how to live, as I was saying, and of myself who knew it and who didn't know what to do with the knowledge, with that knowledge of the life he lived, and who didn't know what to do with me either.

They say that midsummer is on its way, perhaps. I don't know. That the roses are already out, there, at the bottom of the park. That sometimes they are not seen by anyone during their entire life and that they hold themselves like that in their perfume, open, for several days, and then fall to pieces. Never seen by that lone woman who is trying to forget. Never seen by me, they die.

I am in a state of love between living and dying. It is through your lack of feeling that I rediscover your quality: that of pleasing me. I desire only that life should not leave you, otherwise I care nothing for its progress, for it can teach me nothing about you; it can only draw death closer to me, render it more tolerable and, yes, desirable. That is how you stand: facing me, softly, in constant provocation, innocent, unfathomable.

You do not know this.

An Interview with Marguerite Duras
Ana María Moix

A face

The Lover, by Marguerite Duras, begins
with a description of her face. As it was
then, so it is now: a ravaged face, but
beautifully ravaged. This she exhibits
proudly, with dignity, pushing her face
forward, almost offering it to the gaze of
the interviewer, who cannot, fascinated,
tear herself away to observe the room in
which they are now sitting. The room is

in Duras's apartment in Saint-Germain-des-Près, in Paris, on a street nestled between the cafés de Flore and Deux Magots. It's a small room, shining in the pale midwinter sunlight— pale but strong enough to gild the 'used furniture, polished by time' crammed with books and objects collected, not as decorations, but through use and the passing years. And worn down by those years. Everything in the apartment— the windows framed by creepers, the crocheted shawls, the couches seen through half-open doors, covered with silky soft-coloured cushions—everything gives the sense of having been used intensely, almost used to death.

This intense usage, this abuse, is reflected in the face. Like the stranger who approaches Duras in *The Lover,* Duras herself seems to prefer her present face to that of her youth, the face that appears on the book's cover, a stunning photograph of the young Duras.

'Yes, a magnificent cover and a very pretty photograph. But what I don't like is the mouth. So tiny.'

Surely one has to take into consideration the fashion, the make-up of those times.

'Yes, but leaving aside the make-up, after a certain age my mouth grew wider, grew larger.' Duras lays down the book, translated now into a dozen languages after winning the Prix Goncourt. 'Well, the prize was something ridiculous!' she laughs, shrugging her shoulders. 'But what can you do? It was nothing but a whim of theirs, giving me the prize. They carried out their whim.'

Autobiographies

The Lover is impossible to classify. It

can't be called a novel, it can't be called an autobiography....

'No, it's not an autobiography.' Marguerite Duras speaks slowly, in a deep and melodious voice, giving each phrase much thought. She fixes her interviewer with a look that is very much alive, and at the same time, both sympathetic and powerful. 'It is the opposite of a biography. The papers have said that it is autobiographical, but that isn't true, even if that which is told in the text really happened.' She pauses and her eyes seem to smile.

The Sea Wall tells part of the childhood and adolescence reclaimed in *The Lover.* Was *The Sea Wall* autobiographical?

Now the eyes become extraordinarily lucid. 'That was an attempt at autobiography. But *The Lover* is neither autobiography nor confession. The confessional text, Rousseau's *Confessions,* for instance, demands a judgement from the reader. My book demands nothing. There is nothing to judge in it. All the characters are innocent. Does the verb "to innocent someone" exist? I don't mean to declare someone innocent. That's not the same. One declares someone innocent after judging him or her. In *The Lover* no one is judged. The author doesn't judge, she "innocents," she creates innocent characters without pre-judging them. That is why my book isn't a confession. Neither is it a love story. Not at all. The protagonist is not in search of love, she's in search of desire, a desire stronger than herself. And in search of freedom. That's why the mother accepts her behaviour, that's why, all things told, she becomes her daughter's accomplice.'

The Lover's prose is musical, full of repetitions, ellipses, premeditated breaks. That is also Duras's technique in her more recent texts, in *The Slut of the Normandy Coast* and *The Atlantic Man*.

'Yes, there's a musical order to those texts. For me, those books are not literature. As a book, as literature, each of these works doesn't exist. It's only writing. I believe that a poem, if one hasn't set out to "make" it, doesn't exist. Music, on the other hand, exists even if one hasn't tried to make it. In *The Lover* I was swept on by the writing. There was a musical dynamic to it. That was all. Nothing had been planned. I wrote after having been very ill, after an alcohol detox cure, and something happened, something that escaped any possible plan. Maybe it was nothing more than my need to free myself, to free myself at last from literature through literature. To simply attain the writing.'

Her early books responded or seemed to respond to a rigorous plan, to an almost mathematical scheme: *The Square, The Little Horses of Tarquinia, Moderato Cantabile,* titles of the fifties and sixties, when her name was being included (against her will) among the authors of the *nouveau roman*—Claude Simon, Alain Robbe-Grillet, Nathalie Sarraute.

'Yes, those books did respond to a plan, to a rigorous scheme. For instance, *Moderato Cantabile* is divided into six sequences, and each chapter has its order, its distribution, through which the reader can guess that I had studied mathematics. All those are books I wrote on alcohol. In fact I wrote on alcohol in all my books, except *The Ravishing of Lol Stein* and *The Lover.*'

Alcohol and the laws of rigour

The alcohol detox cure took place in 1982; its story is told in an extraordinary book, Yann Andréa's *M.D.* Curiously, the books Marguerite Duras wrote 'on alcohol' are of superb rigour and precision.

'Alcohol is irreplaceable. It's perfect. But it's death. I've almost always written on alcohol, and I've always been afraid. I've always been afraid that alcohol would prevent me from being logical, I've been afraid that it would show in my writing. Now, without alcohol, I'm no longer afraid. But the moment I stopped drinking I was afraid I'd stop writing. The writing in books such as *The Lover* is, as a line by Baudelaire calls it, *"belle d'abandone,"* beautiful in its negligence, in its abandonment, in its loss. ("Seeing you walk to a soft cadence / Beautiful in your abandonment / You are like a serpent dancing / High on the top of a staff.")

'I have no idea if this abandonment has always been within me, forgotten. But it surfaced when I wrote *The Lover*. I wrote it without meaning to write, it happened. I wanted to assemble a photo-album for my son, an album of old photos, photos of myself. And as I began assembling the photos, I also began writing, and suddenly I found myself with a hundred written pages. I wrote over the photographs, I wrote what had taken place and about which I had not written before, a sort of settling of old debts between what had taken place and what I had written had taken place, a settling of old debts between myself and my childhood. I felt like telling the truth because all of a sudden telling the truth seemed like an extraordinary temptation. I didn't think about the style, I didn't think about how I'd write it, and when I started writing I felt that the book itself was the style. I had the impression of not writing at all, I don't remember having "done the writer," as the Italians say. I haven't reread *The Sea Wall*, but I suppose that there I stuck to the rigid laws of the story, to the chronology. I was a manicheist then; the lover could only be ugly and stupid because he paid, he offered money. In *The Sea Wall* I denied that passion of mine for love itself, and I, as a narrator, wasn't present. Instead *The Lover* is me, I'm always present there, me and not my mother, not the brothers, not the Chinese lover. The heart of *The Sea Wall*, which was a political novel, is the capitalist world. The heart of *The Lover* is myself. I am the heart and all the rest of the book, because there's no literature there: only writing. These days no one writes. Or almost no one. There are books, books made out of books, and behind them there is no one.'

Marguerite Duras was born near Saigon in 1914, of French parents, administrators in French Indochina. At the age of eighteen she came to Paris and studied law, mathematics and political science. Her first novel, *Les Impudents,* was published in 1943, followed by *La Vie tranquille* (1944) and

The Sea Wall (1950). The latter became her first critically acclaimed book. By then she had been married twice—to Robert Antelme in 1939 and to Dionys Mascolo in 1942—had had a son, had become a member of the French Communist Party and a contributor to Sartre's magazine *Les Temps modernes*.

'My novel *The Square*, published in 1955, was a Marxist book, a book on the theory of necessities. *The Sea Wall* was a political book. But in my latest work, in *The Slut of the Normandy Coast*, in *The Atlantic Man*, there's a letting go of ideologies, not an abandoned ideology but

rather the other way round: an abandonment of ideology, of all ideologies.'

Fame and death

'I can't understand why *The Lover*
has had such success, has reached a
wider public than my previous books.
I've been launched like some sort of
"star." And I'll tell you something: this
exhibition of my person, this turning
me into something almost sacred, feels
closer to death than anything I've expe-
rienced up to this day. Let me try to
explain. It's something I haven't sought
out, I haven't wished for, and that

77

reaches me suddenly, from outside, just like death. It's something that comes from other people; I receive calls from New York or Tokyo, from a thousand different places, asking me to come for the presentation of my book. This solicitude is an external solicitude, like that of death.'

Is she afraid that this external pressure will influence her future work, or become an obstacle to her writing?

'No, it's not that. Now nothing can influence my writing in that way. Perhaps if this success had taken place when I was in my thirties, it might have been dangerous for my writing, but at my age, no, no longer. What I mean is that this external pressure is like a possession, a perdition that comes from beyond, like death. Now I can hardly go out onto the street, I can't go to a café, I can't go into a bar. Everyone recognizes me, greets me as if we'd been friends all life long. This has nothing to do with the clandestine nature of writing. I can only write for people if I don't know them.'

The very mention of l'Académie Française, the French Academy of

Letters, makes her burst out laughing.

'No, that's impossible! Me in the Academy! The Academy and I have nothing to do with one another, let me tell you. People who know me are certain of that. And I've refused the Légion d'honneur. Just a few days ago someone called from the Ministry of Culture about some medal or other, and no, I wouldn't accept it.'

For many years now the name of Marguerite Duras has been mentioned as a Nobel Prize candidate.

'No, no. Who'd deserve that prize is Nathalie Sarraute, not I. I fought in the French Resistance, I belonged to the Communist Party, I've done things like that all my life. I've been arrested by the police, I've been accused of conspiring against the State, I've been an alcoholic, who knows how many more things like that. I've always been a free person, very free, I've chosen the sort of life that doesn't go with those big prizes, with fine medals. No.'

Her work, both in books and in films, hasn't always been happily received by the critics.

'Critics have never said anything interesting about my work. The best critics of my books are my readers and the people who write to me. The intelligence of certain readers is remarkable.'

At times, Duras has mentioned the discrimination her work has suffered because it was written by a woman.

'They say it isn't true, but it is true. But misogyny is good, a positive thing for women. Yes, certainly, misogyny hides an indifference that is positive for us. It allows us to remain on the margins, to not take part in the game of the male, a game of power. For years now all male discourse has been one same discourse, repeated, repetitive, very much codified, saying one same thing. The only imaginative discourse today is the discourse of women.'

Marguerite Duras had a very peculiar upbringing, part Western, part Eastern.

'France isn't my country. When Mitterand was president, I felt an affinity with this country and its people. But I can't call it my homeland.'

And yet she has travelled extensively through France, and owns several houses throughout the country.

'Yes,' she says laughing. 'And that has been a real problem for me. Because whenever I've had money, I've bought a house somewhere I liked, and then I haven't had enough money to keep it. In Indochina we lived in an administrator's house, and I suppose that this tendency to buy houses is an attempt to regain the house in which I was born.'

Duras has a very extensive *oeuvre:* more than sixty novels, films, plays, books of essays. Does the writing come easily?

'I work a lot, very hard. I've always enjoyed working. Now I work without alcohol. I hope I'll be able to continue to work without alcohol. Because of my liver. I've ended up with a very small liver. That's terrible! Terrible because alcohol is so positive, so perfect, such a major occupation. There is nothing like alcohol. Just look at the drunks in the taverns. They talk to themselves, they are perfectly happy, they are in harmony with their beings. They are like kings. They are the authentic kings of this world.'

Afterword

In France, where popular success is demeaning in the eyes of the intelligentsia, Marguerite Duras has fallen from the grace of the avant-garde. Once the bold scriptwriter of *Hiroshima mon amour,* the controversial novelist of *Moderato Cantabile,* the innovative playwright of *L'Amante anglaise,* the difficult filmmaker of *India Song,* today, thanks to the success of her novel *The Lover,* she is seen by many of the fashionable critics as a mere best seller.

Of course, nothing of that rise in and fall from intellectual esteem seems to make a difference to her work. Her subject, according to Duras herself, was and still is the nature of love. To explore it, she makes use of images, of words, in a book, on the screen, on stage, with no definite limits between one craft and the others. In all she proceeds by paring down the language—visual, written—to the bones, making what she has to say 'explicit without commentary.'

For certain writers (and this may be particularly true of French writers) they themselves are their subject. They are their own stories, language serves to give them an identity. They write, as it were, on a mirror that ceases to make sense without them. In the case of Duras, her self-centred narratives expand in the telling: from a recaptured moment of the past or an examination of the present, she leads the reader into a meditation on language, on the nature of writing or film, on the curious resemblance between the relationships of lovers and the relationships of writers and their public.

In this sense, *The Slut of the Normandy Coast* and *The Atlantic Man* play against one another. In the first,

Duras is the sufferer, fixed at the centre of the emotional landscape; in the second, Duras is the creator, the landscape artist, giving her own story not only a shape and a rhythm, but also a wilful ending. Ana María Moix's interview adds the comments of Duras the reader to this counterpoint of texts.

Alberto Manguel, Sélestat, April 1993

Editor for the Press: Alberto Manguel
Cover Design: Shari Spier / Reactor
Cover Photo: *Shawn, 1988* by Steven Jack
Printed in Canada

Coach House Press
50 Prince Arthur Avenue
Suite 107
Toronto, Canada
M5R 1B5